See the Cat

Three Stories About a Dog

David LaRochelle

illustrated by Mike Wohnoutka

CANDLEWICK PRESS

Story Number One

See the Cat

See the cat.

See the blue cat.

The blue cat is in
a green dress.

The cat's name
is Baby Cakes.

See the blue cat
in a green dress
riding a pink unicorn.

See the red dog.

Story Number Two

See the Snake

See the snake.

The snake is under the dog.

The snake is mad.

The snake is very mad.

The mad snake is going to bite the dog.

The mad snake is
going to bite the dog.

The mad snake is not going to bite the dog.

See the happy dog
wag his tail.

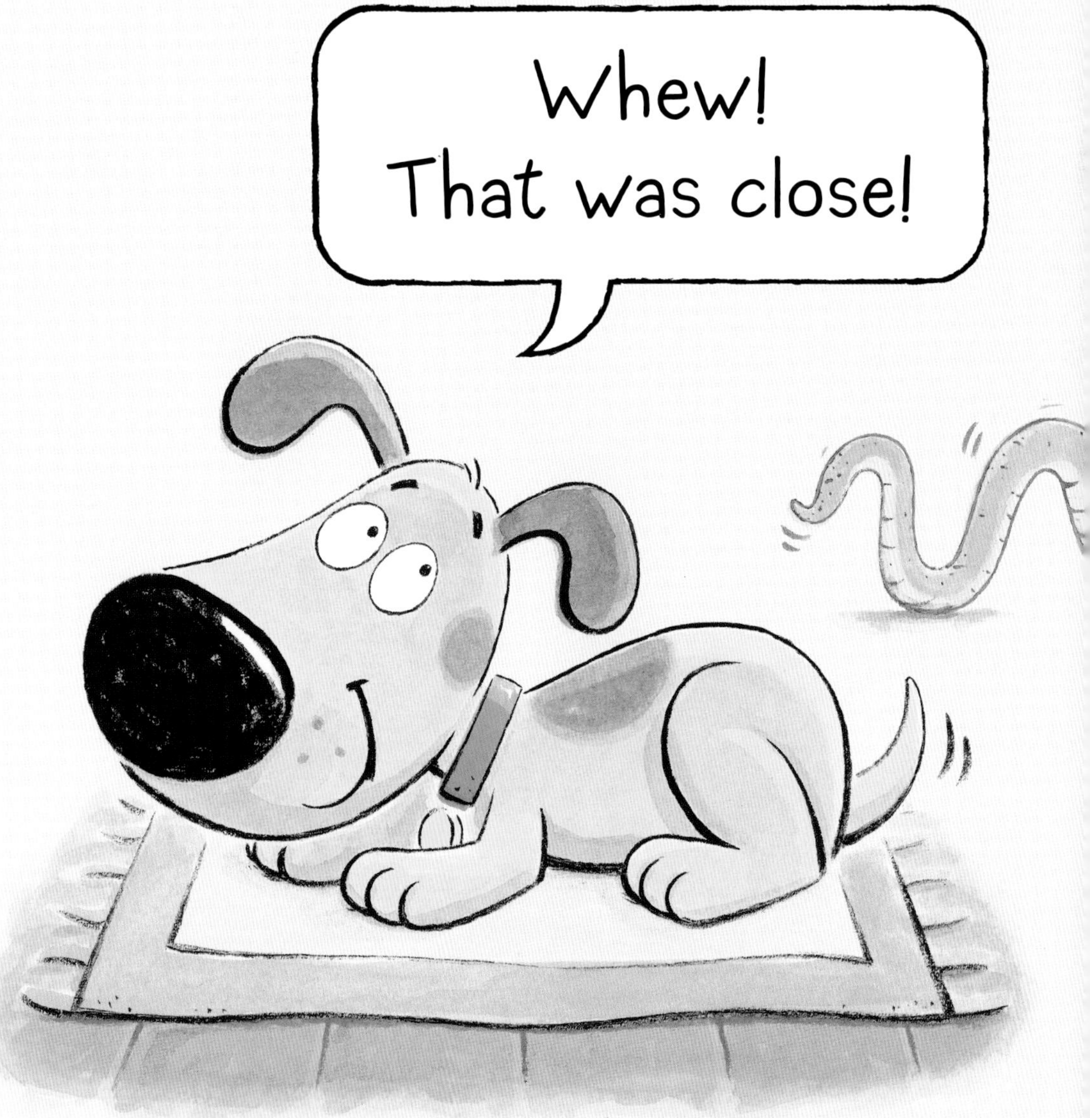
Whew!
That was close!

Story Number Three

See the Dog

See the dog.

See the dog run and jump.

See the dog run and jump
and spin and fly.

If the dog does not
run and jump
and spin and fly,
this hippo
will sit on the dog.

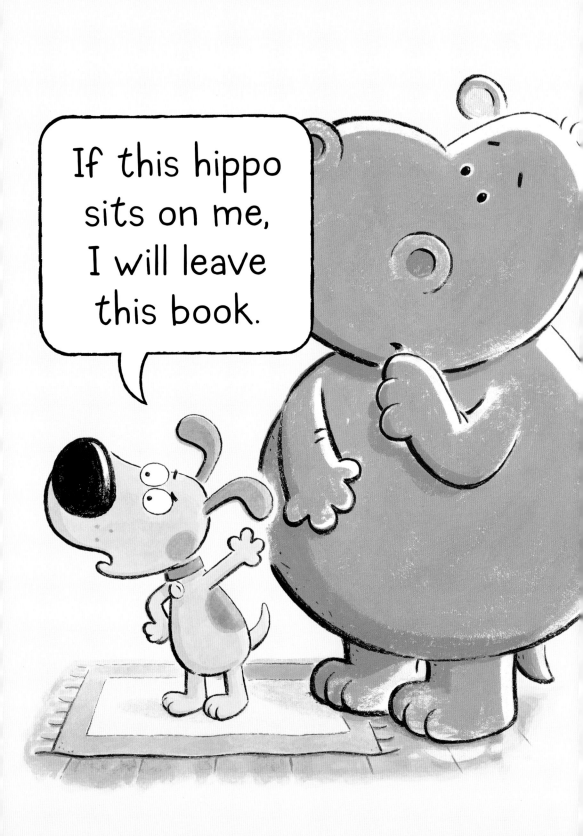

Oh.

In that case, see the dog take a nap.

Sleep well, dog.

To Andrea Tompa, a doggone great editor
DL

To SH, PE, and RS—thank you
MW

First edition 2020

Library of Congress Catalog Card Number 2020915552
ISBN 978-1-5362-0427-8

22 23 24 25 CCP 10 9

Printed in Shenzhen, Guangdong, China

This book was typeset in Myriad and Coop Forged.
The illustrations were done in gouache.

Candlewick Press
99 Dover Street
Somerville, Massachusetts 02144

www.candlewick.com